Mama, Don't Go Out Tonight

BY SALLY GARDNER

R0161753112

W9-BJK-103

BLOOMSBURY
CHILDREN'S
BOOKS

Oriole Park Branch
7454 W. Balmoral Ave.
Chicago, IL 60656

"Mama, Mama,
don't go out tonight."

"You will be all right.
Daisy will be here."

THE CHICAGO PUBLIC LIBRARY

DATE DUE

NOV 2 7 2004		
DEC 2 9 2004		
MAR 1 7 2005		
APR 1 2 2005		
MAY 2 4 2005		
SEP 0 7 2005		
OCT 0 3 2005		
OCT 3 1 2005		
NOV 2 5 2005		

DEMCO 38-296

THE CHICAGO PUBLIC LIBRARY

ORIOLE PARK BRANCH
7454 W. BALMORAL
CHICAGO, IL 60656

DISCARD

To Freya, without whom this book would never have happened.

With love, Mummy

Copyright © 2002 by Sally Gardner

All rights reserved. No part of this book may be used or reproduced in any manner whatsoever without written permission from the publisher except in the case of brief quotations embodied in critical articles or reviews.

Published by Bloomsbury, New York and London

Distributed to the trade by Holtzbrinck Publishers

Library of Congress Cataloging-in-Publication Data

Gardner, Sally.

Mama, don't go out tonight / by Sally Gardner. p.cm.

Summary: A little girl's concerns about her mother leaving her for the evening disappear once she finds out how much fun the babysitter can be.

ISBN 1-58234-790-5 (alk. paper)

[1. Babysitters—Fiction. 2. Mothers and daughters—Fiction.] I. Title.

PZ7.G179335 Mam 2002 [E]—dc21   2002019066

ISBN 1-58234-790-5

First U.S. Edition 2002

Printed in Singapore by Tien Wah Press

1 3 5 7 9 10 8 6 4 2

Bloomsbury USA Children's Books

175 Fifth Avenue

New York, New York 10010

"Why can't I come with you?"

"Because it's nighttime and nighttime is grown-up time."

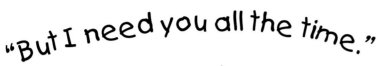

"But I need you all the time."

"I know, sweetie, I know."

"Monster's going to miss you.
Cat's going to miss you."

"The house will feel so funny without you. I am going to miss you so, so, so."

"Give me a kiss now. I have to go."

"Mama, don't go. There's a dragon under the stairs."

"No, sweetie, only the vacuum lives there."

"Mama, you might be kidnapped by pirates."

"Oh, darling, there are no pirates where I'm going."

"Sweetie, don't be silly. No circus would have me!"

"Mama, a giant could take you away and a monster

might eat you up." "I don't think so!"

"The cat could have kittens."

"She's far too old for that."

"Darling, everything is going to be all right.

Give me a kiss! Night-night."

"Daisy, can I have four fishfingers?

One for me and two for Monster and one for my dragon."

"Daisy, shall we go dancing? I will dress up.

I'll be a princess and you can be the prince."

"Daisy, will you read to me? This book and another one.

Is it long now, till Mama is home?"

"Daisy, will you come again? Monster likes you being here,

I like you being here. Daisy, will you sit with me until I go to sleep?"

"Sweet dreams, my sweetheart. Sleep tight."

THE CHICAGO PUBLIC LIBRARY